Thomas in Trouble

Other Books by Andrea Da Rif

Written and illustrated by Andrea Da Rif
THE BLUEBERRY CAKE THAT LITTLE FOX BAKED

Illustrated by Andrea Da Rif
WHERE DID YOU PUT YOUR SLEEP?
by Marcia Newfield

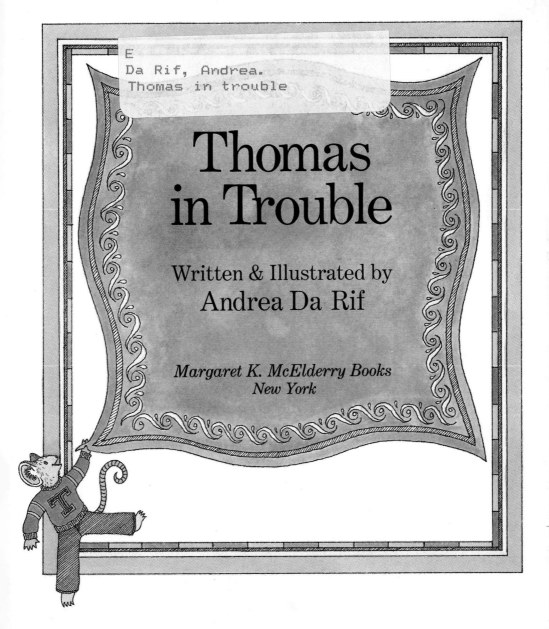

Thomas in Trouble

Written & Illustrated by
Andrea Da Rif

Margaret K. McElderry Books
New York

Margaret K. McElderry Books
Macmillan Publishing Company
866 Third Avenue
New York, N.Y. 10022
Collier Macmillan Canada, Inc.

Composition by Boro Typographers
New York, New York
Printed by Holyoke Lithograph Company, Inc.
Springfield, Massachusetts
Bound by A. Horowitz and Sons
Fairfield, New Jersey

10   9   8   7   6   5   4   3   2   1
First edition

Library of Congress Cataloging-in-Publication Data
Da Rif, Andrea.
Thomas in trouble.

Summary: Thomas runs away from home to escape being punished for getting in trouble, but he brings more trouble on himself than he had in the first place.
[1. Animals—Fiction.   2. Runaways—Fiction]
I. Title.
PZ7.D114Th 1987   [E]   86-10591
ISBN 0-689-50395-4

For all my family

Thomas—T for Trouble—was in trouble again. Two days ago he had hit a baseball through Mr. Owl's window after being warned not to play so close to a house. Yesterday his teacher had made him stand in the corner for talking during math class.

And today, after school, he had dropped a quart of milk and three eggs on the kitchen floor. He was trying to show off a juggling trick for his brother and sister. His mother had had enough.

"Thomas, that's it. No baseball, no television, no cookies and milk for you this afternoon," she said sternly. "You march straight to your room this minute and stay there until I decide you have learned a lesson."

Thomas stared out his window at the lovely spring afternoon. He was mad. Everyone except himself was having a wonderful time outdoors. He thought for a minute. He would run away. It was the only thing to do.

But how? He couldn't go along the road. It passed by the baseball field and his brother would see him. He couldn't go across the back meadow. His mother was gardening and she would spot him. Instead, he decided to sail down the river.

First he would have to build a raft. He searched his room for the things he would need—a jackknife, a bandana, a pack of chewing gum, ten nails and some string. He piled them into his baseball cap, opened his window and climbed out.

He hurried down to the river — and no one
saw him.

Now he had to find some good straight logs. Luckily there were some not far from the riverbank. They were pretty heavy, but Thomas managed to drag them close to the water. He trimmed off all the small branches, tied the logs together with his string and hammered in a nail here and there. Then he stepped back to inspect his work.

The raft looked a little wobbly, and there were a couple of holes between the logs, but after he filled those with chewing gum Thomas thought that his raft looked very shipshape indeed!

He stuck a mast to the deck with another piece of gum and tied his bandana to it to make a sail. And then he was ready to set off! Thomas pushed his raft into the water and jumped aboard.

There was just one trouble. Thomas had no way to steer. And he had not realized how fast the water was flowing. His raft began to go faster and faster. It spun in circles and rocked wildly from side to side. Suddenly it gave one mighty lurch and tipped over!

Thomas was thrown smack into the middle of the river. Now he was *really* in trouble.

"Help! Help!" he cried.

The water was icy cold, the riverbank was far away, and the current was pulling his head under water...

The next thing Thomas knew, he was being
pulled from the water.

"Thomas, are you all right?" cried Mr. Badger as he thumped Thomas on the back.

Thomas nodded slowly, while he coughed and shook the water out of his ears. He was cold and wet and still a bit scared.

"You are very lucky I spotted you. Don't you know how dangerous it is to play around the river? I hope you've learned a lesson," said Mr. Badger sternly. "Now let me take you right home before you catch cold."

"No, no!" exclaimed Thomas quickly. What if they ran into his mother! "Thank you very much, but I'm fine now. I'll go straight home by myself. I promise." And he scampered off before Mr. Badger could change his mind.

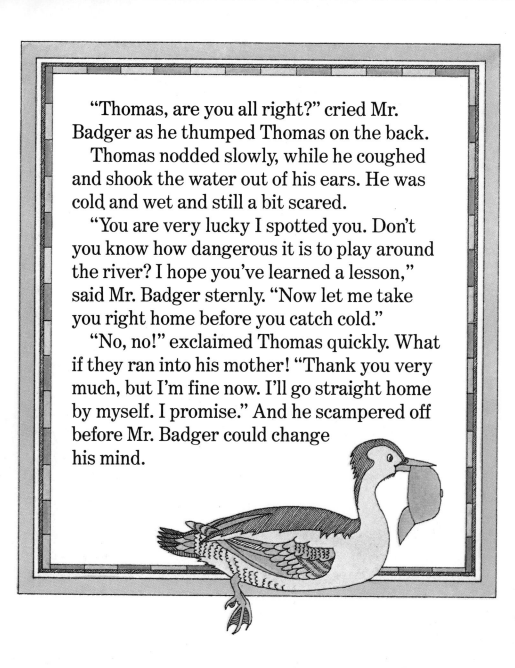

Thomas climbed back into his room. He took off his wet clothes and hid them in a corner of his closet. Then he put on his warmest, coziest sweatshirt and climbed into bed.

He has just snuggled down under the covers and opened a book when his mother peeked around the door.

"Well, I see you've had a nice quiet afternoon for a change." She smiled. "I've brought you a little supper, and when you've finished that, there's a nice full bath waiting for you."

"BATH!" cried Thomas with a jump.

"Is something wrong?" asked his mother. "Oh...no," mumbled Thomas.

"Well then, hurry along. And by the way, I hope you've learned a lesson today about staying out of trouble."

Thomas just nodded.